Snow White and the Seven Dwarfs

Walt Disney's
Snow White and the Seven Dwarfs
An Art in Its Making

featuring The Collection of Stephen H. Ison

A DISNEY MINIATURE

MARTIN KRAUSE

LINDA WITKOWSKI

A WELCOME BOOK

HYPERION

NEW YORK

ISBN 0-7868-6187-8

A DISNEY MINIATURE EDITION

Below and opposite: Doc and Grumpy model sheets, September 28, 1936.

For information address:

HYPERION
114 Fifth Avenue
New York, NY 10011

PRODUCED BY
Welcome Enterprises
575 Broadway
New York, NY 10012

EDITOR
Carol Shookhoff

DESIGNER
Karen Davidson

Printed in Singapore
10 9 8 7 6 5 4 3 2 1

9-28-36

NOTE: DOC IS

Contents

Foreword

I've been asked many times over the years why I decided to collect animation art only from *Snow White and the Seven Dwarfs*. It was never a difficult decision, even in my early collecting days. I always liked the idea that *Snow White* was the studio's first animated feature and felt it was a way of paying tribute to a man I had admired since childhood. Here was a person I never had the privilege of meeting, yet who touched and influenced my life in many ways. I think people need heroes. Walt Disney was mine.

And what better way than this book to honor the hundreds of men and women who spent countless hours sketching at animation tables, exhaustively developing the characters and stories we have come to know and love, and to recognize the many other areas involved in the creative process called animation. Each piece a work of art; each one a moment frozen in time.

Stephen Ison

Overture

*"Mr. Disney has started
a new art that is destined
to go a long way."*

—THE ART NEWS, JANUARY 7, 1933

Movies—whether live action or animation—are literally moving pictures. To create the images we see on screen, lengths of celluloid containing thousands of transparent still pictures pass through a projector at the rate of twenty-four frames per second, fast enough to make each separate frame imperceptible. Whereas live action is broken down into frames, animation builds the illusion of motion, picture by picture, frame by frame.

Opening Credits

*"In [the Silly Symphonies]...
Walt Disney paints a sequence
of movements and resulting
emotional episodes that do
for art what the orchestra
does for music."*

—DOROTHY GRAFLY IN *THE AMERICAN
MAGAZINE OF ART*, JULY 1933

Before *Snow White*, the Disney studio
made only "shorts"—seven-minute,
action-packed, gag-filled cartoons—often
issuing more than one a month. The first
Disney Mickey Mouse cartoon shown in
theaters, *Steamboat Willie* (1928), was a
sensation. It was also one of the first
viable films of any kind with sound
encoded and synchronized on the film
rather than on a separate phonographic
disk, the way in which Al Jolson, in *The
Jazz Singer*, had broken the sound barrier
of filmdom only thirteen months earlier.

Atmosphere drawing for the Silly Symphony,
The Old Mill, by Maurice Noble, 1937.

The advent of sound inspired Disney and his animators to experiment with Silly Symphonies, a new aural-visual experience in the form of musical shorts in color. Sound also led to a new industry standard of projecting twenty-four frames per second instead of the previous sixteen. For live-action pictures, this simply meant additional film. For Disney it meant an increase of nearly 25 percent in the number of drawings needed for the same length of film.

Cel setup for *King Neptune*, Disney's second Technicolor Silly Symphony, 1932.

Disney hired more sound men, musicians, and animators and added more buildings to his studio on Hyperion Avenue in Los Angeles. His brother Roy supplied the financial wherewithal for expansion by licensing merchandise—watches, toys, handkerchiefs, and other spin-offs—bearing the image of Mickey Mouse.

Animation drawing for *Steamboat Willie*, 1928.

13

The Story

"I honestly feel that the heart of our organization is the Story Department. We must have good stories."

—DISNEY MEMO

By 1933 Disney had a formula for a feature. He had the technological edge in sound and color. He had on staff the hit songwriter who wrote "Who's Afraid of the Big Bad Wolf?" He also had the human resources on payroll (including 12 story- and gagmen, 40 animators, 45 assistant animators, 30 inkers-and-painters, a 24-piece orchestra, and 26 technical and support staff members).

From the outset Disney recognized the importance of choosing a subject for his feature that was "known and beloved in practically every country in the world." After considering other stories and fairy tales, in late 1933, the idea of making

CONTINUED —

Snow White the world's first animated full-length feature film began to crystallize in Disney's mind. He vividly remembered seeing a silent-film version of *Snow White* (for which he had saved money from his paper route), but also recognized the practicality of this choice. After the movie opened, he wrote:

The seven dwarfs, we knew, were "naturals" for the medium of our pictures. In them we could instill boundless humor, not only as to their physical appearances, but in their mannerisms, personalities, voices, and actions. In addition, with most of the action taking place in and around the dwarfs' cottage in the woods, we realized that there was great opportunity for introducing appealing little birds and animals of the type we've had success with in the past.

Early gag sketches for the dwarfs by storyman Earl Hurd, 1934 *(left and previous page)*.

Sequence

"I feel that we cannot do the fantastic things based on the real, unless we first know the real."
—WALT DISNEY IN 1935 MEMO TO DON GRAHAM

Disney anticipated the need for new and more skilled artists for the feature (seventy-five were ultimately given screen credit for *Snow White*). He had already started a full-time Disney Art School, with classes held from eight in the morning until nine at night. Don Graham, head of the school, culled new recruits from art schools, who began as "inbetweeners". They drew the interludes between the important points of a character's action which had already been roughed out by the head animator and cleaned up by his assistant.

All Disney artists were strongly encouraged to attend Graham's classes on Walt's time and their own. Instruction stressed line drawing rather than color, and in life classes the artists drew from human models and from animals brought onto the lot. There were regular trips to the nearby Griffith Park Zoo and twice-weekly action-analysis classes, in which short pieces

of live-action film were studied to learn the fundamentals of motion. The purpose of the classes was not to make the artists imitators of nature but to make them such intuitive observers that they could caricature it.

The most important instruction received by the young artists, however, came through their working proximity to more experienced men. The successful inbetweener would become assistant to a head animator, then advance to independent animation.

Preliminary background of the dwarfs' cottage interior by Maurice Noble.

Dwarfs: Inspiration sketches by Albert Hurter *(details)*.

We went to the sound stage...and Walt told us the story of Snow White. It started about 7:30 and went on till 11. We were spellbound. He was all by himself and he acted out this fantastic story. He would become the Queen. He would become the dwarfs. He was an incredible actor, a born mime. When he got to the end he told us that that was going to be our first feature. It was a shock to all of us because we knew how hard it was to do a cartoon short.
—KEN ANDERSON, *DISNEY ARTIST*

The look of the story and of its cast had to be set and story sketches begun. The studio was not departmentalized in those days, and anybody with an idea, a gag, or an inspiration about what a character might look like or do was encouraged to submit it. Bonuses were offered from the outset to encourage such ideas.

Preliminary backgrounds of the dwarfs' cottage by Maurice Noble.

Gag suggestions for Jumpy, Doc, and Bashful by Earl Hurd, 1935 *(overleaf)*.

Storyboard drawing for the "Bed-Building Sequence"
which was ultimately cut from the film.

24

By early 1935, the studio began composing the music, casting for voices, and scripting the picture, which was the necessary prerequisite for layout and animation. The story evolved slowly through a series of conferences attended by Disney, his storymen, and his story sketch artists. They extended the storyline to its full length and then broke it down into sequences and into the general pacing of scenes and camera shots. Each shot was treated in a thumbnail story sketch that roughed out the action of the characters involved, vaguely suggested the setting of the action and footnoted its bit of dialogue. These sketches were then pinned in running order upon a floor-to-ceiling, wall-to-wall storyboard. Drawings could be added, deleted, or changed as ideas came progressively into focus. The storyboards constituted the "script" of the film, from which all the production departments—layout, animation, ink and paint, backgrounds, and camera—would work.

HE SLACKS UP AND VINE SPRINES AWAY FROM POST

LEAVIN

Early gag sketches for the "Bed-Building Sequence."

A LEAF DESIGN, — REPEAT,

Storyboard drawing for the "Bed-Building Sequence," 1937 *(right).*

Animation rough and layout tracing for the "Bed-Building Sequence," 1937 *(opposite and below).*

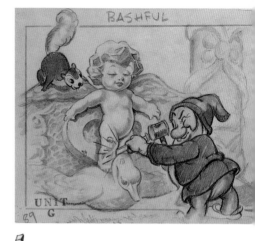

Layout tracing for the "Bed-Building Sequence," 1937.

The standard practice in musicals of the era was to interject songs abruptly into the storyline. Disney himself explained how he wanted certain songs incorporated seamlessly into the action. In a story meeting Walt described the lead-in to Snow White's "Whistle While You Work":

She has seen the cobwebs on the ceiling—everything needs to be dusted—dishes must be washed—then that would lead into the statement, "there's lots of work to do" and into the song. Change words of the song so they fit in more with Snow White's handing the animals brushes, etc.

She might say, "Pots and pans aren't hard to bear"... give brush and pan to squirrels... "If you just hum a merry tune"—and then they start humming...

Get a way to finish the song that isn't just an end... truck out and the melody of "Whistle While You Work" gets quieter and quieter... leave them all working... the last thing you see as you truck away is little birds hanging up clothes... fade out on that and music would fade out.

Cel setup on a preliminary background.

Production

"There could be no compromising on money, talent, or time."

—WALT DISNEY

Cel: ink and gouache on trimmed celluloid mounted to a post-production background (opposite).

Model sketch of Snow White by Grim Natwick, 1935–36 *(overleaf, left).*

Sequence 2B: Scene 2
The Queen on her Peacock Throne. *Cel setup: ink and gouache on celluloid on production watercolor background (overleaf, right).*

With the story progressing, Disney began assembling his production team late in 1935. He brought to the feature his five best directors from the shorts. He divided the characters among four supervising animators. Just as he cast his characters, he cast the animators who would bring them to life. "If he gave Grumpy to supervising animator Vladimir Tytla—Tytla was a grumpy character," says storyman Joe Grant, "whoever did Happy was a happy character. Walt figured it all out for himself." Though Disney recognized the necessity of this division of labor, he remained directly involved with every aspect.

The Disney artists experimented with different conceptions of the characters. The Queen was drawn as a fat, comedic type and as a stately, beautiful type. Snow White herself was modeled by Grim Natwick, who had drawn the character of Betty Boop in New York. Although the Grimm brothers described Snow White as having "hair as black as ebony," early animation models showed her with red or blond hair. Her age also varied between preteen and fourteen, but Disney, recognizing that she would fall in love, decreed that the girl must look old enough to do so.

Rotoscope photograph of the Queen (below) and rotoscope tracing of Snow White (right).

Model sheet, September 28, 1936 (opposite).

The normal human proportion is eight heads tall. Snow White was to be drawn five heads tall. The "human" characters were generally drawn with five fingers, whereas the "non-humans" were given four fingers.

The Disney artists tried a process known as "rotoscoping," or tracing from live-action film projected frame by frame onto a drawing table. While this process seemed theoretically sensible, the difference in proportion of the animated characters to the tracings and the need to exaggerate movement for successful animation meant the rotoscope tracings were of little practical use to the animators, although live film and audio references continued to be used.

"You have to go further than normal to make it seem normal. You have to exaggerate."

—KEN O'CONNOR,
ART DIRECTOR

37

CAST OF CHARACTERS

Snow White:
Janet Gaynor type—14 years old.

The Prince:
Douglas Fairbanks type—18 years old.

The Queen:
A mixture of Lady Macbeth and the Big Bad Wolf—Her beauty is sinister, mature, plenty of curves—She becomes ugly and menacing when scheming and mixing her poisons—Magic fluids transform her into an old witchlike hag—Her dialogue and action are over-melodramatic, verging on the ridiculous.

The Huntsman:
A minor character —Big and tough—40 years old—The Queen's trusted henchman. But hasn't the heart to murder an innocent girl.

The Seven Dwarfs:

Happy:
A glad boy—Sentimental—Addicted to happy proverbs—His jaw slips out of its socket when he talks, thus producing a goofy speech mannerism.

Sleepy:
Sterling Holloway —Always going to sleep—Always swatting at a fly on the end of his nose.

This cast of characters is a preliminary version from a script dated October 22, 1934.

Doc:
The leader and spokesman of the Dwarfs—Pompous, wordy, great dignity—Feels his superiority, but is more or less a windbag.

Grumpy:
Typical dyspeptic and grouch—Pessimist—Woman-hater—The last to make friends with Snow White.

Bashful:
Has a high peaked skull which makes him ashamed to take off his hat—Blushing, hesitating, squirmy, giggly.

Seventh:
Deaf, always listening intently—Happy—Quick movements—Spry.

Prince's Horse:
This gallant white charger understands but cannot talk—Like Tom Mix's horse Tony—The Prince's pal.

Jumpy:
Joe Twerp—Like a chap in constant fear of being goosed—Nervous, excited—His words and sentences mixed up.

Magic Mirror:
The Queen's unwilling slave—Its masklike face appears when invoked—It speaks in a weird voice.

G iven the European origins of the story, European fairy-tale illustrators (such as Arthur Rackham) became the most important design sources for the animators. German influences are evident in the richly carved Bavarian woodwork and hand-hewn furniture of the dwarfs' home. The gnome-like appearance of the dwarves came from Swedish folk imagery.

Preliminary background of the dwarfs' cottage by Maurice Noble.

Detail of production background with painted cobwebs.

W hen a sequence had been storyboarded and okayed it went to the layout department where the picture was to be staged. Character designer Albert Hurter, who gets credit for stylizing *Snow White*, provided the department with inspirational drawings of props, architecture, and backgrounds. Gustaf Tenggren, who came to Disney as an art director in 1936, also began producing inspirational drawings in layout.

The layout artists took these concepts and elaborated them into hundreds of penciled miniaturized sets upon which the characters would act, adding substance to the story sketches. At the same time they made rough layout drawings on which camera mechanics—close-ups, long shots, pans—were diagrammed for use by the animators. These were followed by finely detailed layout designs made as models for background painters and as outlines for animators to plot their scenes.

Master layout drawing of a
trail through the mountains.

While a character was evolving from clean-up animation to the painted cel, the background artist began working on the production background for the scene. As many as 729 different backgrounds were required for *Snow White*, so the color schemes and overall tone had to be carefully planned and followed to achieve visual uniformity. Disney had strong opinions about color:

We want to imagine it as rich as we can without splashing color all over the place. I saw Harman-Ising's cartoon about Spring ...last night. They got colors everywhere and it looks cheap...It's just poster-like. A lot of people think that's what a cartoon should have. I think we are trying to achieve something different here....We have to strive for a certain depth and realism...the subduing of the colors at the right time and for the right effect.

Production background, 1937.

The premiere was set for December 1937; the animators were still drawing in September. Most of the backgrounds were approved in August, September, October, and into November. During these months, nearly everyone was working fifteen-hour days. By October, the final two links in the production chain, ink-and-paint and camera, were working in shifts around the clock.

Preliminary background of the dwarfs' bedroom by Maurice Noble *(above)*.

Sequence 4C: Scene 15
Cel setup of the dwarfs' bedroom *(right)*.

Given that the smooth-surfaced cel sheet was the eventual support for the painted characters, the paints needed special components to help them adhere readily as a uniform layer to the cel. It couldn't bead up or crack away from the cel before it was photographed. It had to be flexible when it was applied, couldn't cake excessively, and had to be brushable. The exact formulas remain studio secrets to this day.

High-quality drafting skills, exacting fluidity, and neatness were essential when inking the cels, especially since, in the final projected film, the character outlines were magnified many times on the movie screen. Experience proved that women were neater and more consistent as inkers and painters than men.

The studio had 178 painters who wore white cotton gloves to keep the painted cels clean and unscratched. They completed as many as 21 cels per eight-hour day.

Detail of a cel setup with added water special effects cel.

Color model cel (*opposite*).

If one woman had painted all of the Snow White cels in gouache at the studio's estimated average rate of 17 cels a day, or 1.1 feet of film, it would have taken her 1,490 weeks, the equivalent of 29 years.

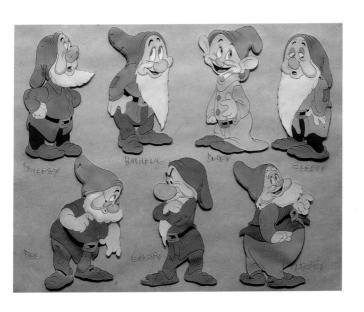

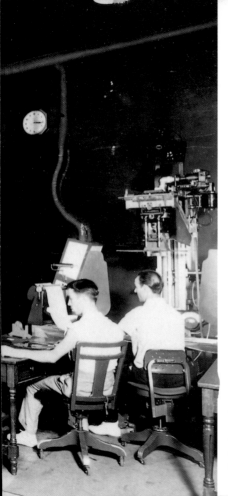

From the initial story sketches to the production background and the painted cels, over 2.5 million pieces of art in some form—all done by hand—were required to create the eighty-three minutes of *Snow White and the Seven Dwarfs*. The results of the coordinated efforts of the storymen, layout and background artists, animators, assistant animators, inkers, painters, and cameramen speak for themselves to all those who view the final product.

The camera room at Hyperion studio in 1937, with multiplane camera at left and standard animation camera.

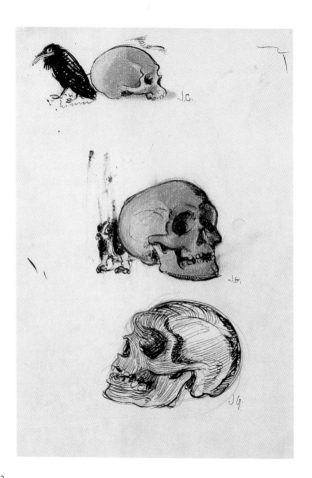

In all, 750 artists are said to have contributed to *Snow White* between 1934 and 1937, making it the largest collaborative art project ever undertaken in the United States. The feature was dubbed "Disney's Folly." Time and money were in short supply, yet Disney was constantly upgrading the project.

Character model sketch of the raven *(opposite)* and original inspiration sketch for the Witch *(below)* by Joe Grant, 1936.

Money problems became critical in mid-production in 1937. Disney recalled the situation years later:

My brother Roy told me that we would have to borrow another quarter of a million dollars to finish the movie. I had to take the bits and pieces [of completed film] to show to the bankers as collateral.... On the appointed day, I sat alone with Joe Rosenberg of the Bank of America, watching those bits and pieces on a screen, trying to sell him a quarter of a million dollars worth of faith. He didn't show the slightest reaction to what he'd just seen. He walked out of the projection room, remarked that it was a nice day, and yawned! Then he turned to me and said, "Walt, that picture will make a pot full of money."

Atmosphere watercolor of the Queen's laboratory by background painter Maurice Noble.

E ven with the deadline looming, Disney made alterations in the final months of production. He had a natural feeling for what ought to be in the story, adding and subtracting scenes to advance the plot. In the case of one addition he explained: "When Snow White and the dwarfs are having that entertainment, and she's singing 'Some Day My Prince Will Come,' the audience will want that to last forever, because the Witch is coming!"

Animation drawing (*above*).

Cel: ink and gouache on trimmed celluloid mounted to wood veneer post-production background (*right*).

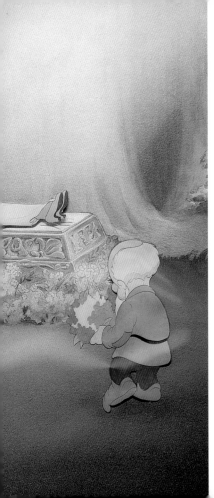

At the premiere Disney noted a practically imperceptible jitter as the Prince bent to kiss Snow White. He wanted it fixed. According to a contemporary account in *Liberty*, "even after the film was running in New York, he was still working on new animation for the Prince. He sent it on too, and made the theaters use it."

**Sequence 16A:
Scene 5, no. 63**
Animation drawing by Grim Natwick *(above)*.
Scene 1
Cel setup: ink and gouache on celluloid on production watercolor background *(left)*.

Epilogue

"Best film of the year."

—THE FILM DAILY

The premiere at the Carthay Circle Theatre on the evening of December 21, 1937, was a gathering of Hollywood's glitterati—Chaplin, Garland, Barrymore, Gable, and Lombard. The anonymous makers of the film mingling among them—storymen, layout artists, background painters, and animators—could not know how the audience would react. As animator Ward Kimball remembers the evening:

Clark Gable and Carole Lombard were sitting close, and when Snow White was poisoned, stretched out on that slab, they started blowing their noses. I could hear it—crying—that was the big surprise. We worried about the serious stuff and whether they would feel for this girl, and when they did, I knew it was in the bag. Everybody did.

HIS FIRST FULL LENGTH FEATURE PRODUCTION!

The dwarfs sing their marching song on the way to work.

Snow White window bill
designed by Gustaf Tenggren.

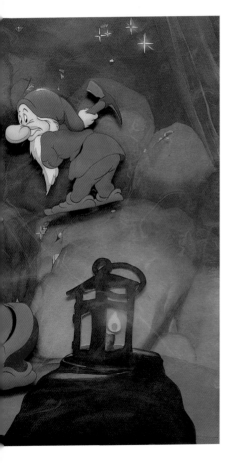

Disney had invested $1,480,000, more than four times the average cost for a feature film in 1937. And just as Disney's banker had predicted, it made a whole "pot full of money." Estimates based on both foreign and domestic releases placed *Snow White*'s revenues for 1938 at ten million dollars, making it the most successful film of its time.

Sequence 4A:
Scene 6
Cel setup: ink and gouache on celluloid on production watercolor background.

HIS FIRST FULL LENGTH FEATURE PRODUCTION
Walt Disney's
Snow White
and the Seven Dwarfs
in the Marvelous
MULTIPLANE TECHNICOLOR
©W D P
Distributed by RKO Radio Pictures, Inc.

WALT DISNEY PRESENTS

Snow White and the Seven Dwarfs

Supervising Director
David Hand

Sequence Directors
Perce Pearce
Larry Morey
William Cottrell
Wilfred Jackson
Ben Sharpsteen

Story Adaptation
Ted Sears
Otto Englander
Earl Hurd
Dorothy Ann Blank
Richard Creedon
Dick Rickard
Merrill De Maris
Webb Smith

Supervising Animators
Hamilton Luske
Vladimir Tytla
Fred Moore
Norman Ferguson

Animators
Frank Thomas
Dick Lundy
Arthur Babbitt
Eric Larson
Milton Kahl
Robert Stokes
James Algar
Al Eugster
Cy Young
Joshua Meador
Ugo D'Orsi
George Rowley
Les Clark
Fred Spencer
Bill Roberts
Bernard Garbutt
Grim Natwick
Jack Campbell
Marvin Woodward
James Culhane
Stan Quackenbush
Ward Kimball
Wolfgang Reitherman
Robert Martsch

Character Designers
Albert Hurter
Joe Grant

Art Directors
Charles Philippi
Hugh Hennesy
Terrell Stapp
McLaren Stewart
Harold Miles
Tom Codrick
Gustaf Tenggren
Kenneth Anderson
Kendall O'Connor
Hazel Sewell

Backgrounds
Samuel Armstrong
Mique Nelson
Merle Cox
Claude Coats
Phil Dike
Ray Lockrem
Maurice Noble

Songs
Frank Churchill
Larry Morey

Music
Frank Churchill
Leigh Harline
Paul J. Smith

Gustaf Tenggren's poster design, 1937.

Sequence 1B: Scene 3A

Master layout: graphite on off-white paper. This opening scene was described as a "fade in from a long shot" on the final draft script of January 5, 1937. With the perfection of the multiplane camera later that year, it became a multiplane shot heightening the illusion of penetrating into the scene.

"Magic Mirror on the wall, who is the fairest one of all?"

Sequence 1B:
Scene 4
Animation drawing: graphite heightened with red and green pencil on off-white wove paper.
Animator: Art Babbitt *(opposite)*.

Scene 10
Animation drawing: graphite and red pencil on off-white wove paper.
Animator: Art Babbitt *(near right)*.
Cel: ink and gouache on trimmed celluloid mounted to post-production airbrushed background *(far right)*.

Sequence 2A:
Scene 17
Cel setup: ink and
gouache on celluloid
on production water-
color background
(above).
Scene 1
Cel setup: ink and
gouache on trimmed
celluloid mounted to
post-production
airbrushed background
(left).

"We are standing by a wishing well."

Sequence 2A: Scene 18
Cel setup: ink and gouache on celluloid on production watercolor background with watercolor-on-paper overlay.

"I'm wishing."

Sequence 2A:
Scene 9 *Cel setup:* ink and gouache on celluloid on production watercolor background *(below top)*.
Scene 12 *Rough layout:* graphite heightened with blue and red pencil on off-white paper *(below bottom)*.

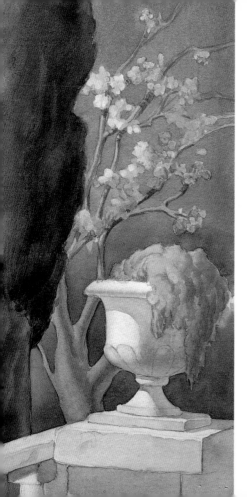

"I have but one song..."

Sequence 2A:
Scene 24
Animation drawing: graphite, red and green pencil on off-white wove paper.
Animator: Grim Natwick *(above)*.
Scene 29
Production background: watercolor on white paper *(left)*.

75

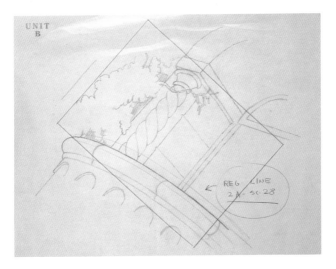

← REG-LINE
2A-SC-28

"...only for you."

**Sequence 2A:
Scene 28**
*Layout tracing with
camera mechanics:*
graphite and red
pencil on off-white
wove paper *(above).*
Scene 31
Animation drawing:
graphite over red
pencil on off-white
wove paper.
Animator: Grim
Natwick *(left).*

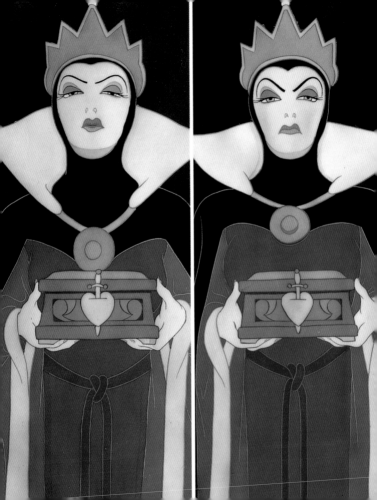

*"Bring back her
heart in this!"*

**Sequence 3A:
Scene 2**
Cel: ink and gouache
on trimmed celluloid *(right).*

**Sequence 2B:
Scene 8**
Cels: ink and gouache on
trimmed celluloid mounted to
post-production airbrushed
background *(opposite).*

Sequence 3A: Scene 9A
Cel setup: ink and gouache on celluloid on production watercolor background with watercolor-on-paper overlay. This background was also used for scenes 8, 8B, and 10.

81

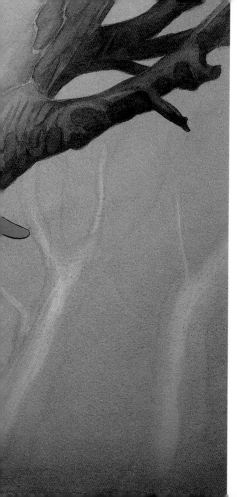

*"Run child!
Run away!
Hide! In the
woods!"*

**Sequence 3A:
Scene 17A**
Cel setup: ink and
gouache on celluloid
on production water-
color background.
This is the earliest
production back-
ground in the Ison
Collection. It was
okayed for camera
and stamped "August
19, 1937," just four
months before the
premiere. The latest is
stamped "November
18, 1937" (Sequence
3A: Scene 48).

Sequence 3A:
Storyboard drawing:
graphite on off-white
wove paper.

85

Sequence 3A:
*Preliminary
background:* water-
color on off-white
wove paper *(above).*
Rough layout:
charcoal and red
pencil on buff
wove paper *(right).*
Art director:
Gustaf Tenggren.

Sequence 3A:
Scene 48
*Special effects
background:* oil on
white wove paper
(above).
Scene 49
Animation drawing:
graphite strengthened
with red and blue
pencil on off-white
wove paper.
Animator: Jack
Campbell *(opposite).*

"Please, don't run away."

Sequence 3B: Scene 7
Animation drawing:
graphite heightened
with red and green
pencil on off-white
wove paper.
Animator:
Eric Larson.
Larson's
"scramming"
animals were
animated on one
cel level, while
Ham Luske's
Snow White, in
their center, was
animated on
another.

*"With a smile
and a song."*

**Sequence 3B:
Scene 14, nos.
24 and 33**
Animation drawings:
graphite over red
pencil on off-white
wove paper.
Animator: Ham Luske
(opposite top and left).

**Sequence 3C:
Scene 2Bx**
Rough layout:
graphite on
off-white paper.

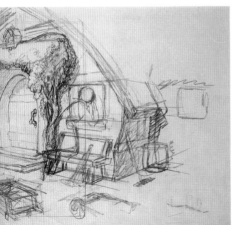

"Just like a doll's house."

Sequence 3C: Scenes 2Ax–2Bx, and 3
Production pan background: watercolor on
white paper *(continued on next page).*

"Oh, it's dark inside."

Sequence 3C: Scene 2B

Cel setup: ink and gouache on celluloid on production water-color background. To simulate Snow White wiping the window, John Hubley hand-wiped each cel in this scene when it was on the camera stand.

**Sequence 3D:
Scene 3A**
Cel setup: ink and
gouache on celluloid
on production water-
color background.

"Look at that broom!..."

**Sequence 3C:
Scene 13**
*Production pan back-
ground:* watercolor on
white paper *(above)*.
This background
appeared on screen
for three seconds in a
pan shot from left to a
stop at right. The
distorted drawing of
the stool and flagon
simulated the visual
effect of a quickly
panning camera.

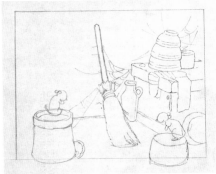

"...They've never swept this room."

**Sequence 3C:
Scene 13**
*Preliminary
background:*
watercolor on
white paper *(left)*.
Background artist:
Arthur Fitzpatrick.
Layout tracing:
graphite on
off-white paper
(opposite bottom).

"You do the dishes…" Sequence 3C:
Scenes 22, 24, and 26

Cel setup: ink and gouache on celluloid on production pan background in watercolor *(continued on next page).*

"...and I'll use the broom."

Only a still shot of the right section (Scene 22) remained in the film.
The pan shots of Snow White sweeping in Scenes 24 and 26 were
deleted, according to the final draft script.

"If ya dig, dig, dig with a shovel or a pick in a mine, in a mine…where a million diamonds shine."

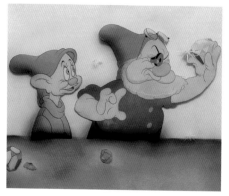

Sequence 4A:

Layout: graphite and ochre pencil on off-white paper *(left).*

Scene 11

Cel: ink and gouache on celluloid *(opposite bottom).*

Scene 3

Cel setup: ink and gouache on celluloid on production water-color background *(below left).* Cel of Grumpy is key to this background, but the cel of Dopey is not.

Sequence 4A:

Scene 10 *Animation rough:* graphite and ochre pencil on off-white wove paper. *Animator:* Fred Moore *(above).*

"Heigh Ho, Heigh Ho..."

Sequence 4A:
Scene 16
Production background:
watercolor on white
paper.

"...it's home
from work
we go."

**Sequence 4B:
Scene 5**
*Preliminary
background:*
watercolor on
white paper.

111

"Door's open!
Chimney's smokin'!
Somethin's in there!"

Sequence 4D:
Scene 8
Cel setup: ink and
gouache on trimmed
celluloid on prelimi-
nary watercolor
background (*below*).

Sequence 4D:
Scene 16
Storyboard drawing with camera mechanics: graphite and red pencil on off-white paper.

(14) "DOC" WATCH EVERY MOVE"

"It's up there. In the bedroom."

Sequence 5A:
Scene A1
*Production
background:*
watercolor
on white paper.

115

> "Jimminy crickets! What a monster!"

Sequence 5A: Scene 2
Layout: graphite on off-white paper *(right)*. *Cels:* ink and gouache on celluloid *(below and opposite)*.

116

"Why, they're
little men!"

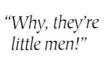

"Why wash? What for?"

Sequence 5B: Scene 6B
Cel setup: ink and gouache on celluloid on production watercolor background.

119

"We ain't goin' nowhere."

Sequence 5B: Scenes 13–13B and
Sequence 5A: Scenes 38E, 41A, and 43A
Cel setup: ink and gouache on trimmed celluloid on
production pan background in watercolor *(below)*.
The cels are not key to the background, which was
painted for the fight between Doc and Grumpy
(Sequence 5A, Scenes 36–46), but was cut late in
production.

**Sequence 5B:
Scene 13B**
Animation drawing:
graphite over red
pencil on off-white
wove paper.
Animator:
Frank Thomas.

"So splash all you like."

Sequence 6A: Scene 12
Cel setup: ink and gouache on celluloid on production watercolor background *(above).*

"Get him over to the tub!"

Sequence 6A: Scene 16A
Animation drawings: graphite over red pencil on off-white wove paper *(opposite bottom).*

Scene 24 nos. 5A and 9
Animation drawings: graphite over red pencil on off-white wove paper *(top and bottom left).* Animator: Vladimir Tytla.

"Get the soap!"

**Sequence 6A:
Scene 24A**
Cel setup: ink and
gouache on celluloid
on production pan
background
in watercolor *(above).*

**Sequence 6A:
Scene 24A, no. 21**
Animation rough: graphite
over red pencil on off-white
wove paper *(opposite)*.
*Animation clean-up with
color notations:* graphite with
red and green pencil on
off-white wove paper *(right)*.
Animator: Vladimir Tytla.
Color notations were added by
the ink-and-paint department
with reference to the 1,500
numbered tints created for the
feature in Disney's paint lab.

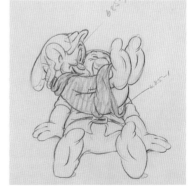

125

"I've been tricked!"

Sequence 7A: Scene 4
Cel setup: ink and gouache on celluloid on production watercolor background.

"I'll go myself to the dwarfs'
cottage in a disguise so complete
no one will ever suspect."

Sequence 7A: Scene 9 *Cel setup:* ink and gouache on celluloid on production pan background in watercolor *(above)*.
Scene 5 *Trial cel, repainted:* ink and gouache on celluloid
(right). Animation drawing: graphite and red pencil on off-
white wove paper *(opposite).* Animator: Robert Stokes.

128

"Now a formula to transform my beauty into ugliness."

Sequence 7A:
Scene 9B *Cel:* ink and gouache on celluloid *(right).*
Scene 21 *Cel with lighting effect:* ink and gouache on celluloid *(below).*
Animation drawing: graphite over red pencil on off-white wove paper.
Animator: Art Babbitt *(opposite).*

> *"To age my voice,*
> *an old hag's cackle."*

Sequence 7A: Scene 11C
Cel setup: ink and gouache on celluloid on
production pan background in watercolor *(below)*.
Layout with camera mechanics: graphite and red
pencil on off-white wove paper *(right)*.

"To whiten my hair, a scream of fright."

"And now a special sort of death for one so fair. . . . What shall it be? Ah! A poison apple."

Sequence 7A:
Scene 12
Production vertical pan background: watercolor on white paper *(right).*
Scenes 19 *(opposite top),* 31 and 31B *(opposite bottom)*
Cel setups: ink and gouache on celluloid on production watercolor background.

Entertainment

**Sequence 8A:
Scene 13**
Cel setup: ink and
gouache on celluloid
on production
watercolor
background.

137

Sequence 8A:
Scene 13 *(opposite)*
and Scene 24 *(right)*
*Rough layouts: ochre
pencil strengthened
with graphite and red
pencil on off-white
wove paper.*

*"Some day
my prince
will come."*

Sequence 8B:
Scene 10,
no. 41
Animation rough:
red pencil on off-
white wove paper.
Animator: Grim
Natwick.

140

Sequence 8B: Scene 10, nos. 61 and 77
Animation rough: red pencil strengthened with graphite on off-white wove paper. *Animator:* Grim Natwick.

*"You're sure
you'll be
comfortable?
Well, pleasant
dreams."*

"A fine kettle of fish!"

Sequence 8C:
Scene 18
Animation drawing: red pencil strengthened with graphite on off-white wove paper. *Animator:* Grim Natwick *(opposite top).*
Scenes 18 and 20
Production background: watercolor on white paper *(opposite bottom).*
Scene 24
Cel setup progression: ink and gouache on celluloid on production watercolor background with watercolor-on-celluloid overlay *(right).*

"Dip the apple in the brew..."

"...Let the Sleeping Death seep through."

Sequence 9A:
Cels: ink and gouache on trimmed celluloid mounted to post-production airbrushed background.

"The little men will be away,
and she'll be all alone."

Sequence 10B: Scene 1
Cel setup: ink and gouache on celluloid on production pan
background in watercolor *(continued on next page).*

Sequence 10B: Scene 3

Rough layout: graphite and red pencil on off-white wove paper *(inset).*

**Sequence 13A:
Scene 6**
Cel: ink and gouache
on trimmed celluloid
(opposite).
Scene 5
Preliminary background:
watercolor on
white paper *(top).*
Production background:
watercolor on
white paper *(right).*
The word "flour"
on the bowl was
airbrushed out
in anticipation
of foreign language
releases of the film.

"Mmmm. Makin' pies?"

Sequence 13A: Scene 4
Production background:
watercolor on white paper.

Sequence 13A: Scene 13, nos. 60 and 106
Animation drawings: graphite and red pencil with green pencil shadow indications on off-white wove paper. *Animator:* Norm Ferguson.
These drawings were later autographed by Joe Grant, character model designer of the Witch.

Sequence 13A: Scene 18
Layout drawing: graphite and red pencil on off-white wove paper. Scene 18 was deleted from this sequence.

"Shame on you for frightening a poor old lady."

Sequence 13A: Scene 22A

Production background: watercolor on white paper. Cels of the birds are from Sequence 3B and are therefore not key to this background.

"Hey! Look!"

**Sequence 14B:
Scene 6**
Cel setup: ink and
gouache on celluloid
on production pan
background in
watercolor.

**Sequence 14F:
Scene 2**
Animation drawing:
graphite over red
pencil on off-white
wove paper.
Animator: Robert
Stokes *(left)*.
Scene 3 *Cel:* ink and
gouache on trimmed
celluloid *(below)*.

**Sequence 14H:
Scene 1** *Cel:* ink and
gouache on trimmed
celluloid *(opposite)*.

*"Now take
the apple,
dearie,
and make
a wish."*

160

"I wish..."

Sequence 14G: Scene 5
Cel setup: ink and gouache on celluloid
on production pan background in watercolor.

**Sequence 14 J:
Scenes 22–27A**
*Layout inspiration
sketches:* charcoal
heightened with white
on off-white paper.
Art Director:
Kendall O'Connor.

*"I'm
 trapped!"*

**Sequence 14J:
Scenes 22–27A**
*Layout inspiration
sketches:* charcoal
heightened with
white on off-white
paper.
Art Director:
Kendall O'Connor.

167

**Sequence 14J:
Scenes 28** *(left)*
and 29 *(above)*
Cels: ink and gouache
on trimmed celluloid
mounted to post-
production airbrushed
backgrounds.

The Sleeping
Death

**Sequence 15A:
Scene 8**
Animation drawing:
graphite, red and
blue pencil on
off-white wove paper.
Animator: Milt Kahl.

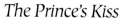

The Prince's Kiss

Sequence 16A: Scene 5, nos. 30 and 63
Animation drawings: graphite strengthened with
red and green pencil on off-white wove paper.
Animator: Grim Natwick.

**Sequence 16A
Scene 6
nos. 4, 14, 33, and 37**
Animation clean-ups:
graphite and red
pencil on off-
white wove paper.
Animator:
Grim Natwick.

**Sequence 16A
Scene 11A
nos. 8, 14, 24, and 34**
Animation clean-ups:
red pencil on off-
white wove paper.
Animator:
Grim Natwick.

"And they lived happily ever after."

Sequence 16A:
Scene 13
Cel: ink and gouache on celluloid *(above)*.
Scene 15
Cel: ink and gouache on celluloid *(opposite)*.

177

Animation Art

Cel animation uses transparent sheets of cellulose nitrate or cellulose acetate ("cels") as the drawing surface. These sheets are placed individually atop a drawn or painted background and photographed sequentially; when projected at twenty-four frames per second—the standard speed in the 1930s—the character seems to act in a landscape.

Pages 178-185: The animation process from the animator's "roughs" to the cel setup. Reconstruction of the steps in production by Linda Witkowski with permission from the Walt Disney Company.

Background: initial line tracing.

Animator's "rough" drawing.

Clean-up drawing.

Background: watercolor rendering.

Inked cel.

Painted cel.

Overlay: initial line tracing.

Animator's "rough" drawing.

Clean-up drawing.

Overlay: watercolor rendering.

Inked cel.

Painted cel.

Painted cel with
added special effects.

Painted cel with
black shadow cel.

Glossary

animation:
the process of creating motion from frame-by-frame techniques in film-making. In cel animation, animated characters are first drawn on paper and then traced and painted onto cels. The painted cels are then placed over a background and photographed one frame at a time. When the completed film is projected at a rate of twenty-four frames per second, the illusion of motion is created.

animator:
an artist who, in rough form, creates the extreme drawings of the character action for a scene.

assistant animator:
an artist who cleans up the animator's rough drawings. At times the assistant animator may also draw some of the inbetweens for a scene, leaving any remaining drawings for the inbetweener.

background:
a finished rendering from the final layout drawing that provides the setting for the character action and, if necessary, special effects.

cel level:
the order and number of levels (A–D and, in extreme cases, E) initially indicated on the animation drawings, in which the character cel

and/or special effect cels are to occur per frame of action. In some instances different portions of a character's action are broken down into different levels.

cel setup:
a setup that consists of the production background, on top of which one to four layers of cels are registered, and that constitutes the elements of a scene as it would be seen in one frame of film.

cel:
shortened term for celluloid. See "celluloid."

celluloid:
a thin sheet of clear cellulose nitrate (or, since the early 1940s, cellulose acetate) on which

the character or special effects are painted. The painted cels are then placed over the background as they would occur per frame of film and photographed one frame at a time. Several cels are therefore photographed sequentially over one production background.

character color:

the specific range of colors for a character that are painted onto the back of the cel.

character outline:

the linear line on the front of the cel denoting the forms and shapes of the character.

checker:

the person who checks all the completed elements of a scene against the notations on the corresponding exposure sheet to insure that everything is correct for the camera.

clean-up/ clean-up animation:

the process of converting the rough, sketchy animation drawings into smooth, clean lines by retracing each animation rough onto a new piece of animation paper.

color model cel:

painted character cel that shows the colors for a given character. The color model cel is used as an aid in finalizing the character colors for a scene and determining the colors for the production background of that scene.

color model drawing:

linear drawing of a character on animation paper in which the specific colors for that character are indicated.

color separation lines:

lines initially made on the clean-up animation drawings with different color pencils to indicate areas in which a different color ink line is to be used by the inker when he or she traces the outline of a character onto the front of the cel.

color study:

see "preliminary background."

dailies:

the filmed portion of a scene that is processed the previous night by the laboratory.

director:
the person in charge of the various production stages of a feature.

drawing level:
see "cel level."

drawing numbers:
the sequential numbering of each animation drawing for a scene. These numbers correspond to the numbers written for each frame of film on the exposure sheet for that scene.

exposure sheet:
a form in which the dialogue, character, and special effects action, cel number and level, as well as notations for the camera are indicated per frame of film for a given scene.

extremes:
animation drawings indicating the extreme points of character action.

field line:
a rough linear line along the sides, top, or bottom of the cel that indicates the parameters for the colors of a character. This line is applied to the front of the cel when the inker traces the character outline from the clean-up drawing.

field:
the area of a scene that will be in view when photographed by the camera.

final layout:
see "layout."

inbetweener:
an artist who creates the drawings that occur between the animator's extremes and any other

drawings done by the assistant animator.

inbetweens:
animation drawings indicating the character action as it occurs between the extremes.

inker:
the person who traces the outline from the clean-up drawing onto the front of the cel with ink.

inking:
the process of tracing with ink or thinned paint the character outline, object, or special effect onto the front of the cel by hand.

key setup:
see "cel setup."

layout:
a drawing showing the scale, perspective, and elements of a

background.
The size of the characters and their path of action are also indicated on the layout. Initially the layout is drawn in rough form. Once the character action has been okayed for clean up, a final layout is created in accurate detail.

let-down:
a calculated darker and grayer color value that, when painted onto a cel, compensates for the graying and increased density of each cel level created when one to four cels are placed on top of one another per frame of film.

mask cel:
a cel in which a portion is painted with black paint—with either a brush or airbrush. The mask cel is placed over the portion of

a background or character that is in shadow and photographed with the corresponding cels and back-grounds at a portion of the total time necessary for that scene.

master background:
see "production background."

model sheet:
a sheet of paper on which different views of a character are illustrated. The model sheet serves as a guide for the animator and assistants to the appearance and construction of a character.

moviola:
a projection machine used by the animators to view pencil tests.

overlay:
separate areas in the foreground of a scene behind which portions of the character action occur. An overlay may be painted onto a separate piece of paper, glass, or cel.

painter:
the person who paints colors onto the back of the cel.

painting:
the process of applying the character colors onto the back of the cel by hand.

pan:
the process in which the camera appears to move horizontally or vertically across a scene. This sense of movement is accomplished by moving the elements of a scene in one direction under the camera.

peg bar:
a metal (or, more recently, plastic) bar with a series of small pegs. All the animation paper, cels, and background art are punched with holes that correspond to the peg system, which supports the artwork and keeps it in registration throughout the stages of production.

pencil test:
the process of photographing frame by frame the rough and clean-up animation drawings for a scene in order to critique the pencil animation for smoothness when the film is projected. To save printing time and expenses, the pencil tests are viewed in their negative form—white pencil lines against a black background.

preliminary background:
moderately rendered backgrounds that are painted with the selected colors for a scene as a color study for the production background.

production background:
a painted background used in the production of an animated film. Also, see "background."

rotoscope:
a machine that projects live-action film footage onto a drawing table one frame at a time so that the image can be traced onto animation paper. The resulting rotoscope tracings served as guides from which the animator created lifelike movement.

rough layout:
see "layout."

roughs/rough animation:
the process of creating a series of rough, sketchy drawings that indicate the character action for a scene.

scene:
a portion of a film that depicts one situation.

self-ink lines/ self-lines:
see "color separation lines."

sequence:
a series of related scenes that, combined, depict a portion of the story.

soundtrack:
that portion of a film comprised of voices, music, and sound effects.

spacing chart:
a simple graphlike diagram made by

the animator, usually in the bottom right corner of the drawing, to indicate the number and spacing of drawings that are to occur between the extremes.

story reel:

the timed, filmed version of the story sketches in order, enabling the director to have an early understanding of the sequence and total length of the animated feature.

story sketch:

a sketch, often drawn on animation paper, that depicts a portion of a story.

storyboard:

a large cork board to which story sketches are pinned in comic strip fashion in an order that tells the complete story.

sweatbox:

a small room in which portions of a film are viewed for critique.

synchronization:

when the sound and picture elements of a film are occurring in unison.

thumbnail sketch:

a very rough drawing that is one to three inches in size.

trace-backs:

the portion of a figure that does not move on the screen and is traced from a previous drawing onto one or more consecutive cels by the inker.

truck:

the process in which the camera moves toward or away from the elements of a scene.

working reel:

a working copy of the film, begun by photographing the story sketches on the storyboard for each scene. These scenes are spliced together in their proper order to illustrate the film in rough form from beginning to end. As a scene is completed in rough animation, it is filmed and put into the working reel in place of the corresponding filmed story sketches. This replacement process continues with each scene through rough and clean-up animation, as well as with the painted cels and back-grounds, until the entire film is completed in color.